GREETINGS FROM GRAVIPAUSE

a novel

BRIAN BRADFORD

Jaded Ibis Press
sustainable literature by digital means™
an imprint of Jaded Ibis Productions
Seattle • Hong Kong • Boston

For my daughter Erin
(the *Bup*)

"Perhaps stars have no option but to fall from the sky... But people—
the man and the woman, you and I—we build bridges and destroy
them and build them again.

Chasms gape.

Things fall in.

The shoulders we hold—or release—are so warm."

—*Debra Di Blasi, from "Thaw"*

"Don't ask me to make sense of this whole damn mess. I have no answers for you. I guess it's just one of those things, ya know?"

—*From a note written by my father, left on the kitchen table. October 22, 1966. Jersey City, New Jersey*

Greetings From Gravipause

gravipause *(grav e poz) n. (1) In cosmology, gravipause marks the point in space between two celestial bodies where the gravitational field of one celestial body ends, or is neutralized by that of another. (2) A place where the ties that bind have become frayed and are of little consequence. (3) The postcard reads* Greetings From Gravipause.

I remember moments of soft silence, and nights when I lay unsuspecting in the black leather harbor of TV room sofa while my wife, a direct descendant of Tojo, loomed low off my starboard bow. She zeroed in before diving kamikaze into my soft unguarded underbelly.

Bonzai!

A direct hit.

Bonzai!

The carnal flames rising.

Bonzai!

Left me a twisted wreck.

Yes, there was a time in our marriage. A time not long ago. A time when we were *infamous* together.

But now it's Sunday morning. A different kind of silence. Obdurate. Cold. We sit at the kitchen table where she has wrapped herself in Biore Strips. And I can do no more than hold silent vigil. My tee-shirt-belly billowing out over my boxer shorts like a spinnaker sail, insides cauterized by Mount Gay rum. My wife lifts her teacup with both hands.

"Used to," she says, "you was kakkoii to jihatsu-teki" (Japanese for *cool* and *spontaneous*). "Now you is futoi to musekinin' na" (Japanese for *fat* and *irresponsible*).

And I search through my limited arsenal of words, search for something with sharp edges that I can fire across at her and, if my aim is true, cut a hole right through her. But nothing comes to me. And I feel betrayed by the silence, the slow burn of Mount Gay, eleven years together, Sunday morning.

"Whaddya want to do today," I ask as I pour another rum.

"Don't know," she says, as she stares at the wall behind me, "what will *we* do?"

1.

Still Life With Man Leaving. Jersey City. October 22, 1966. A little after 5 in the a.m. He rises. Casts off his tee shirt. Walks to the window, and presses a calloused hand against the cool glass, removes it and smiles to himself, smiles at the ghost handprint that he leaves. Is leaving. Her. As she sleeps.

The quilt encased terrain of her body. Hip a soft mesa. The valley of her midriff leading up in a delicate slope to her small shoulders and that great plain that stretches out across the bed where he did lie now empty. And he feels it, becomes that emptiness. Moves to the dresser where he lights a Camel. White smoke encircling his head as he sees himself plain in the mirror. Takes a drag off his cigarette. Bare-chested now he looks like a tired Whitey Ford.

"Wait," she says her voice thick with sleep, "I'll get up and make the coffee."

"No," he says without turning around, "you go back to sleep. I'll see you later."

And he realizes that this is the last lie he will ever have to tell her. October 22, 1966. A little after 5 in the a.m., with morning moving against the bedroom window. A ghost handprint on the glass. He pitches the cigarette with thumb and forefinger, puts on a clean tee shirt and leaves the room.

The Boulder/Osaka Express
(An Exploration of Angular Distances)

Scale of Angular Distances: *When viewing the night sky with the naked eye it is important to keep in mind that space is not a fixed, linear plane. Locations of stars and other celestial bodies are measured in terms of relative arcs and angles. This "angular distance"—stated in degrees—is never exact, but approximates for celestial observers the relative distance between waypoints.*

I have always been a few degrees off when trying to fix my sight on the precise point in time that I fell in love with her. I trace the arc that somehow links who I was with what we've become. Eleven years of marriage. But I struggle these days to connect the dots—those waypoints that first led me to her. A very distant constellation. The Boulder/Osaka Express.

B/O EX 1: I am a failed bulimic. Unable to subscribe to the less than subtle verities of *purge* I live my life in a chronic state of *binge and binge.* Thighs, tits, soft chairs, empty highways, cabernet, Pouilly-Fuissé, mangoes, Macanudos, beer, boats, brats on the grill, Fellini, fettuccini with white or red clam sauce, jazz, dope, Ellen Barkin, secrets, kudos, Klieg lights, a standing ovation every time I walk into the Trident to buy my morning papers, headlines, skylines, mashed potatoes and gravy, belly, more belly, ragtops, long hair, money and sneakers that don't fall apart. It is all about appetites. Mes chers collègues. Boulder, Colorado. September 21, 1989. Appetites.

B/O EX 2: Having completed my dissertation—A *Libretto for Pulsars* —I sink into a deep and anxiety-ridden depression. My breasts swell and begin to ooze a viscous lacteal emulsion. I experience episodes of intense but controlled rage. These are augmented by violent mood swings and feelings of abject despair. I am suicidal. Colleagues at the CU Graduate School of Arts and Sciences assure me that this is a common phenomenon, "PhD postpartum," they say. No longer able to cope, I seek out the services of a local shaman. He lives in a one room flat above the New York Deli on Pearl Street and bears an uncanny resemblance to the actress Esther Rolle. After several hours of incantation and laying crystals, he prescribes a strict regimen of valerian root and chocolate-covered biscotti. My condition improves steadily with time but my dissertation which proffers the argument that there *is* sound in deep space—that radio waves emitted from pulsars are actually select arias from Puccini operas (think of *Un bel di Verdremo*; now think of *Un bel di Verdremo* piped through the galaxy keeping the cosmos jumping)—is summarily dismissed and I am forced to take a job as a bartender at Juanita's (Authentic Mexican Fare at Family Friendly Prices).

B/O EX 3: I come into a rather large sum of money betting against the Denver Broncos in successive Super Bowls. I put most of the money in T-Bills and. with what is left, I purchase a 1970 Buick LeSabre ragtop and a pair of Ray-ban Wayfarers. Years later I will draw on this windfall to buy a house in Cranford, New Jersey, 07016. A modest Cape with hardwood floors and an indefatigable front lawn.

B/O EX 4: Standing in line at Carvel late one afternoon early one evening, enveloped in a cocaine–anejo haze, I come to the sudden and acutely devastating realization that the Santa ice cream cake on display is actually a Fudgie the Whale ice cream cake turned on its head and refinished with a faux Santa veneer. I see this as a sign, a powerful metaphor for the decay and imminent collapse of Western Society as we know it. "Sprinkles?" the thin-lipped girl in the Crayola-red smock asks from behind the louvered panes. She is holding my vanilla swirl cone on high and, with her hair pulled back from her face and dupe pad in hand, she looks like a sleep-deprived incarnation of the Statue of Liberty. "Sir," she persists, "chocolate or rainbow?" "No," I say in a loud and steady voice as I come to realize that my time in Boulder, Colorado has all but exhausted itself. "No sprinkles today, sweetheart!" I am an expatriate.

BO/EX 5: *Adieu,* Boulder, Colorado. In an effort to cut all the earthly tethers that tie me to Boulder, Colorado, I steal my neighbor's .30-06 and assassinate my Acme Juicerator with the citrus attachment. I bury the shell casings in my backyard, along with my Birkenstocks, mullet, patchouli tinctures and autographed picture of Stephen Hawking. Two days later I am arrested, arraigned and temporarily detained at the Boulder County Jail. Back on the street, conspiracy theories abound as I make bail—rumors begin to surface intimating that I was not the lone gunman. With the law closing in, I ride the

RTD local to Denver, make a brief stop at El Chapultipec for jazz and green chili, then board an ANA red-eye to Osaka. The Boulder/ Osaka Express.

B/O EX 6: Arriving at Itami Airport I am unmercifully beaten about the head and body with the word Gaigin (*outsider*). At the baggage carousel I pluck my portmanteau from the revolving skids and try to compose myself. I am tired and frightened and desperate for something familiar as I seek temporary asylum in a nearby men's room only to find that the Japanese toilet has not yet fully evolved, is nothing more than a ceramic basin sunk flush to the dirt begrimed floor. No seated commode. No American Standard here in the Land of the Rising Sun. And yet, I had no idea how this moment would serve as my initiation into what Huntington calls the *nuance of cultural diversity.* Staring down at that Japanese toilet, I experience yet another in a series of odd epiphanies. Years later I will fold this experience into an epithet— *that sonofabitch is lower than a Japanese toilet*—which I still use but reserve for the truly reprehensible: a guy who sleeps with his best friend's wife, TV evangelists, Reagan Democrats, realtors, auto mechanics, most cops, and anyone who has ever remotely considered naming his first born *Ignatius.*

B/O EX 7: First impressions of Japan: One can purchase tall cans of beer from street vending machines here without fear of judicial or tribal censure. In many respects it is a far more enlightened culture than its contemporaries.

B/O EX 8: Standing at Shinsaibashi beneath a spray of neon, watching almond-eyed girls in silk kimonos, I am suddenly abducted by a cadre of renegade Mormon Missionaries. I'm taken to a climate-controlled self-storage dump where I am forced at gunpoint to eat lime Jell-O and watch Donnie and Marie re-runs. Months into my captivity I am introduced to Mulekite, chief inquisitor and promulgator of thought reform for the paramilitary arm of the Church of Latter Day Saints. We spend countless hours reading aloud from *The Book of Mormon* and playing cribbage. I take from him: a clearer understanding of the "Articles of Faith" and a renewed respect for polygamy. He takes from me: the ability to cheat at cards without fear of divine reprisal. Several months pass. Back at Shinsaibashi I am pimping for the LDS, bringing lost sheep back to the fold. At night I teach conversational English at America Eigo Gakuin, a storefront juku owned and operated by deposed capos of the Gambino crime family. Class repeat after me: "Badda bing, Badda beep, Badda boop, Badda bing, Badda beep, Badda boop, Badda bing, Badda beep, Badda boop—Fuggeddaboutit!"

B/O EX 9: August 6, 1991. That's when I first laid eyes on her. The dark-haired girl who would one day become my wife. She was leaning against a poster of an aging Akira Kurosawa at the Kotobuki Theater as strangers filed out of his *Rhapsody in August.* Call it odd coincidence, call it serendipity (something I would come to not only trust but expect later in life), but I would see her again that night on the platform at Namba Station and we would ride the train back to Kaizuka together and go for coffee and walk until the street lights timed out, and the next morning she would feed me shiso leaves and daikon and play the koto and sing as we sat on a stone bench in her father's garden. August 6, 1991 I met a dark-haired girl who was funny and hopeful and a whole lot prettier than an aging Akira Kurosawa.

BO/EX 10: "Aishiteru yo" (I love you).
"Aishiteru wa" (I love you, too).
One night on the beach at Kada - July 6, 1992.

B/O EX 11: I am a failed Mama's boy. Standing on the platform at Namba Station again, waiting for the train I begin to feel that familiar vertigo, dizzying, delicately debilitating as I push myself closer to the platform's edge, fix my eyes on the rails bending into the rain-soaked darkness. I am waiting for her, the ancestral daughter of a Ueki-Ya (traditional Japanese gardener), mezzo soprano, the dark-haired girl who has fast become the center of my universe. It is then that I feel the unmistakable, umbilical tug at my middle. My mother, thousands of miles and a short cab ride away, has finished her morning tea and is now standing on her back porch in Bayonne, New Jersey, reeling me in as if I am some sort of fleshy kite.

"I told you," she says, "I did *not have* you to have you play house on the other side of the world."

"We'll be back for the holidays," I say, "you'll meet her then."

"Oh, will I?"

Yes."

"So, they celebrate Christmas over there?"

"Sort of."

"What do you mean *sort of?*"

"Well, sort of..."

"She Catholic, at least?"

"Buddhist."

"Oh, really."

B/O EX 12: Sayonara Osaka. We went to Kada that night, the night before we were to leave Japan. A typhoon was whining its way north from Shirohama and the beach was empty. Waves jumped at the jetties as thunderheads gathered above. When the sky opened up and wind torqued the rain and sand into a full-on tantrum, we took cover in an abandoned bungalow. That night we talked about what the future would bring, as shutters slapped applause against the clapboard siding like great wooden hands, and gulls danced an unsteady hornpipe in the rafters. When the storm had cleared, she made her way down to the surf alone and stared motionless at the sea and the dark clouds as they continued on toward Kobe. I knew then that she was saying goodbye. Goodbye to the beach at Kada and more. Goodbye to those people she loved and all the things she had come to know. I made many promises that night. Some I would keep.

Origami

My wife's fingers are slender gods as they move together in spaces filled with quietude—folding a page from an old diary that she brought with her from Osaka: flat—lifeless—paper—folding—her past—folding—paper.

"Look," she says when she is finished "this is tsuru *(crane)*," and she places the tiny paper bird in my hand. "This tsuru is Japanese bird of fortune and happy life."

And I'm not quite sure I understand, understand what it is that she has given me. And that could be part of the problem. These days. I stare down at my own hands, a network of fractured routes and wonder if these are the hands of my father.

2.

Stockings. There are things that he learned to accept about his life—other things he learned to ignore. Small tempests in his head that came on with little or no warning drove him to rye whiskey and, what's worse, made him a slave to his own indifference. October 22. 5:24. He feels the cool tile bless the bottom of his bare feet as he stands before the mirror over the sink. In the glass he sees her stockings draped, deflated on the rod above the tub. She is everywhere. In places where she has no business. Every time he hoists a mail sack, kites a check, raises a double VO to his lips, he feels her presence dragging him down. At times it is all he can do to keep his hands busy while the larger part of him—something that remotely resembles a conscience—does penance for all the things he's done and all the things he's failed to do. Even here in one of the few quiet places in his noisy and all too crowded life she is with him. Her stockings on the rod above the tub like the discarded skin of a sweet and bitter fruit for which he never truly acquired a taste.

In another part of town Madeline is waking up.

Work
(parts I & II)

Retrograde Motion: *This "backward" motion of planets occurs as a result of relative velocity. Planets following their orbital pattern—generally west to east—may appear to be moving contra-orbital when in fact they are moving at a higher rate of speed within a tighter orbit, thus creating the illusion of backward or retrograde motion.*

Working at Frankie Shine's Candlelight Inn
Truckers Welcome (part one)

K-Chit K-Chit K-Ching
K-Chit K-Chit K-Ching

There is an old tin ceiling in Frankie Shine's Candlelight Inn Truckers Welcome. An old tin ceiling that has been painted the color of tapioca pudding. Frankie says, "It lightens the place up. Gives the joint a touch of class." And he should know. Every year he trades in his old Caddie for a new Sedan DeVille, fully loaded. Every Sunday he takes his wife, who is also named Frankie, to Monmouth to play the ponies. She sips champagne cocktails and smokes her Cartier Vendome Lights right down to the filter while Frankie handicaps long shots. "Only the best for me and the wife, kid. Gotta be the Clubhouse," Frankie says, "You can keep the Grandstand. That's for hand jobs, every garbage pail lining the street!"

K-Chit K-Chit K-Ching

K-Chit K-Chit K-Ching

Frankie inherited the Candlelight Inn from his father, Frankie Senior. Back then it was a saloon. Back then you could get beer a nickel a glass, 35 cents a pail. And the old man, Frankie Senior, always made sure that there was plenty of food, free food–cold cuts and potato salad and jars of pickled eggs on the bar for his patrons who were mostly truckers and longshoremen. "Drinkin' man's gotta eat," he'd say. But that was many years ago. Back when a saloon was... a saloon.

K-Chit K-Chit K-Ching

K-Chit K-Chit K-Ching

When Frankie Senior died there was a line of semis in the funeral procession that stretched from the saloon to the Holy Name Cemetery. Two weeks later Frankie Junior raised the drink prices and did away with the free lunch (except for the pickled eggs, which to this day still permeate the air like Eau de Secaucus). He placed a hand drawn sign behind the bar which read PLEASE TAKE OFF YOUR CAP WHEN DRINKING IN THIS ESTABLISHMENT and covered the tables with linen cloths which he ordered from his second cousin—Frankie from Bayside. "It's mauve," he would say as he held up a napkin. "The wife picked out the color. Gives the joint a touch of class."

K-Chit K-Chit K-Ching

K-Chit K-Chit K-Ching

I started working for Frankie Shine when I got back from Osaka. Call it a rare moment—a nebula which vaguely resembled my own sense of responsibility aligned with a planet-sized desire to get me and my wife off of my mother's couch and into our own apartment—that moved something inside of me, brought me to the Candlelight Inn one afternoon.

Frankie was sitting in a corner booth, reading the *New York Post*.

"What the hell were you doing in Japan?" he said, "I hate those slanty eyed bastards. Can't trust 'em."

"I married one," I said.

"That's different. I was talking about the *men*—it's the Japanese *men* you can't trust. Little yellow savages. The women is another story... I heard if you got one of them Jap *ladies* you got it made. Heard they do whatever you say."

"I guess so," I said.

"Know how to make a Negroni?"

"Campari, gin, sweet vermouth..."

"Not bad, kid, not bad."

K-Chit K-Chit K-Ching

K-Chit K-Chit K-Ching

There is an old Burroughs cash register at Frankie Shine's Candlelight Inn Truckers Welcome. Wood and brass. And whenever a shot and beer goes out over the metaled bar that register rings out *K-chit K-Chit K-Ching*. And sons of truckers and sons of longshoremen and other guys some of them named Frankie or Nicky or Stash sit with their caps off and drink the afternoon down.

K-Chit K-Chit K-Ching.

And Allison waits tables here and the guys at the bar, some of them named Buddy or Jimbo or Jesus, keep a close watch as she bends to place a bar napkin on the linen tablecloth and her shirt hangs open just enough and one time this London-Fog-Wall-Street-Journal type comes in and orders a Charles Dickens Martini (*no Olive-or-Twist—get it!*) and says to her "Baby, I'd love to get into your pants." And she places the martini down without spilling a drop, answers, "Already have one asshole in my pants—what on earth would I do with another?"

K-Chit K-Ching.

But it's Friday night here at Frankie Shine's Candlelight Inn Truckers Welcome. And someone is going on about dem Yanks, dem Yanks, and dem Yanks. And the jukebox, an old Rockola Princess is fighting for her life–it's A8–it's Patsy Cline, *Crazy... crazy for being so lonely.* And one old timer is out to cadge a drink and Frankie Shine nods him one over on the cuff, sits at a corner table keeping an eye on things, reading his racing forms like Buddha in an Armani shirt (fell off the truck, kid, know what I'm sayin').

K-Ching.

And I'm here, behind the bar, drinking it all in and have been for nearly eleven years, but you know it's only a temporary gig. A way to pay the bills until something more permanent comes along and to tell you the truth I don't mind it all that much anymore—spending my time spilling whiskey and making cigarette change and the regulars here they seem to like me OK and they call me *professor* and tip me well and Allison, too. She calls out another drink order, "Two Buds, two Lights, shot of Rumple and a Remy neat."

K-Chit K-Chit K-Ching.

Later when it slows down a bit and Frankie goes home for dinner Allison and I do a shot together, something sweet, and she tells me that she is home alone for the weekend and asks me if I want to drop by after we close up and sometimes I do. I go with her and don't feel all that guilty about it. Not that guilty at all.

K-Ching.

Closing Time (part two)

Another night. I wipe down the stainless steel bar top, oil the mahogany, drag the mats out back. Allison sits on a barstool, counts her tips as I clean the speed rack and put the bottles back.

"I'm going to the diner for coffee," she says "Want to come with?"

"Nah," I say, "not tonight." I cash out her charge tips and walk her to her car.

The night sky is still as I move across the empty lot. I'm sitting on a curb a little after 3 a.m. when it occurs to me that I am exactly where I am supposed to be. Alone. Adrift. Another odd epiphany: It's decisions I've made that have placed me in this tight orbit— eleven years of marriage, drunken Sundays, an empty parking lot at 3 a.m. and what's worse, woefully worse, is that I have come to accept it.

Back inside I put the barstools up, turn the neon beer lights off and mix myself a VO Manhattan, easy on the vermouth, easy not to bruise my whiskey. I put another dollar in the juke. C17. And Sinatra eases out something about the *old ennui.* Closing time at Frankie Shine's Candlelight Inn Truckers Welcome. Turn out the lights. Lock the door. Go home to the wife.

3.

Whiskers in a Basin. Out of the shower, a towel wrapped around his waist, he swirls badger hair bristles in an Old Spice shaving mug, lathers warm soap on his face and neck. A mist rises in the bathroom as tiny tributaries cut their way down the length of the mirror above the sink. The scent of bay rum fills him for a moment, takes him away, away to that place where a man goes when he comes to realize that the days ahead are as scripted and certain as the days gone by. But things would be different now.

He slides the razor from its ivory handle, cuts a clean lane along his jaw line. He is thinking about Madeline, thinking about how he left her that first night after making love. Him standing on the corner, staring up at her bedroom window waiting for the light to go out.

She said, "you can't you afford to have me in your life."

He said, "I can't afford not to."

He cuts tiny circles in the warm water–soap and whiskers–wipes the blade clean on a towel draped across his shoulder, turns his whitewashed cheek to the mirror. And she comes to him again. In a back booth at Ruther's, a juke joint on West Side Avenue. Madeline. She is crying. And he is easily taken in by her tears. A young waiter brings two highballs on a tray. The room is dark.

She said, "I don't know if I can stay in this. Not the way it is..."

He said, "The way it is—is not forever."

The cool bite of blade on skin brings him back. He rides it gently over the cleft in his chin, then with short strokes takes the stubble above his lip. The hiss of bathroom radiator. A morning ritual. A man shaving. A man who will leave everything behind today for a woman twelve years his senior, a woman he hardly knows, but knows deep in that place where a man can get lost, that place where the past and the future just don't seem to matter– knows that he is going with her.

"I'll meet you in the alley at seven," she said. "Make sure you park around the block, behind the deli. Don't keep me waiting."

"When have I ever kept you waiting?"

He cups his hands beneath an open spigot, washes residual soap from his face and neck, pulls the rubber stopper and watches the water eddy into a tight spiral. Out. Patting his face dry, forsaking the talcum powder. A morning ritual. A man standing before a mirror— again. A man casing the days ahead, reading whiskers in a basin as if they were tea leaves at the bottom of a seer's cup.

The Neighborhood

Galaxy: *There are approximately 200 hundred billion (200 X 10) stars in our galaxy, 750 billion to one trillion solar masses—these include stars, planets and diffuse nebulae. This community of solar masses is known as the Milky Way, a large spiral galaxy located 2.9 million light years from Andromeda (M13). Our solar system is situated on the outskirts of this symmetry plane, some 20 light years above the Galactic Equator.*

I hate my neighbors. Jimmy and Jamie. I hate the way they exaggerate that *eeee* at the end of their names, mug for the camera when there *is* no camera, and introduce themselves while waiting in the checkout line at the supermarket or perhaps the receiving line at the Annual Rotarian/Junior League Hot Plate Charity Ball. "Hi, I'm Jim-*eeee* and this is my wife, Jam-*eeee*, care to buy a raffle ticket?"

I hate my neighbors and I especially hate them on the weekends. I hate the way they watch me when, on rare occasion, I defy gravity and from the perilous height of a fully extended aluminum ladder, subject myself to the muck and indignity of cleaning the gutters. I hate the way Jimmy's voice rings out from below as buoyant and cheery as a major 7th chord. "Hey, Wallenda, when you get done up there you *must* come over and sample some of my latest. I've got a really heady Dunkelweizer and I just bottled a nice raspberry lambic, *do* come over and bring the wife."

"No thanks," I say, "too fuckin' busy."

"Perfectly fine, he says. "Perfectly fine. Perhaps another time."

I hate my neighbors. I hate the fact that they hold hands and go for walks on Sunday afternoon, and that Jimmy owns every tool known to man—from adz to zax—he's got 'em all and what's worse, he knows how to use them. I hate that they say things like "do come over" and "perfectly fine." As if anything can actually be *perfectly fine*. It makes about as much sense as a pandemic strain of incurable syphilis being described as *mildly catastrophic*. And did I mention that Jimmy works for Good Humor Ice Cream? "Assistant Regional Director of our northeast franchises," he beams (and I mean this in the most literal sense of *beam*) "and product development," Jamie finishes his thought. She is beaming, too. And what more can I do amid all this beaming than hang my head and pray for rain.

The Salad Days

Before we bought into the neighborhood my wife and I bivouacked in a tiny loft above the Dixon Pencil Factory on Tonelle Avenue, Jersey City. I remember hot summer nights and making love to the dissonant music of an old GE fan that oscillated in the window, a relic left from days gone by. I remember how the graphite fog hung still in the air, covering everything in a soft gray veil. It was like living in an old 50's sitcom. Grainy. Black and White. We were *I Love Lucy* with just a hint of nihono youna (*Japanese flavor*).

MEET THE WIFE: A coquettish, geisha wannabe with angelic

mezzo soprano pipes.

AND HER HUSBAND: A 30-ish, Anglo underachiever with delusional dreams of one day becoming a noted cosmologist/professor of astronomy.

A ZANY ROMP: They were young and horny and covered in the residual dust of a million Number 2 Dixon pencils.

The Realtor

The realtor who sold us on the neighborhood was a large, pear-shaped woman, more Anjou than Bosc if memory serves. She wore a fist-sized, rhinestone-encrusted seahorse brooch on her lapel and smelled of cooked turnips. It was during this time that I had managed to amass no small amount of

A. The Elusive Spondulics

B. Filthy Lucre

C. Geld

D. The Long Greens

working as an adjunct instructor of astronomy at Wood Hills Community College, and as a bartender at Frankie Shine's Candlelight Inn Truckers Welcome. Padding my tip jar. Hoarding the money I made selling anabolic steroids to the local PAL Youth Football program (a story that will receive further attention at another time) and with the biennial windfall I previously spoke of—betting against Denver—was able to raise enough dough for a down-payment.

"Lovely, lovely, lovely," the pear-shaped woman said as she led us through the modest cape with wrap-around back deck and feracious front lawn, "the perfect starter home for young marrieds."

205 South Union Avenue

"Lovely, lovely..."

The neighborhood.

"Just a five minute walk from downtown and the nearest elementary school. And the neighbors—well, lovely, lovely, lovely."

I must admit that I still think of that realtor these days whenever I idle by some roadside fruit and vegetable stand or when somebody at the table orders Mont Blanc with Poached Pear for dessert. I think of her with disdain, her silly *lovely, lovely* refrain and fecund turnip effluvium.

The Variance

Here's Jimmy, standing on our front porch one night ringing the doorbell, ringing the doorbell in a cold merciless rain.

And me peeking out through the blinds, smiling at Jimmy standing there. In one hand he is holding the salad crisper that his wife borrowed several weeks ago, in the other an envelope. He rings the bell. I walk slowly toward the mud room.

"Hi neighbor," he says, "sure is a wet one." Jimmy shamelessly displaying an acute sense of the obvious.

"Indeed," I say.

"Here's that crisper. Sorry we had it so long." Jimmy burping the salad crisper, handing it to me.

"Listen," he says as he raises the envelope, "my wife and I would like to put a foyer" —which he pronounces *foy-yay*— "at our side entrance and the town issued this variance because of the property lines. Sorry about all the foofaraw but it would really help us out if you would sign it so I could start construction."

He hands me the envelope.

I retreat back into the mud room, muttering *foy-yay... foofaraw... foy-yay... foofaraw... foy-yay... foofaraw.*

Jimmy offers me a pen, a Conway Stewart fountain pen (British luxury. Solid gold or platinum. Your signature deserves no less). I put the pen in my shirt pocket and watch a drop of rain snake down the flat plain of Jimmy's cheek. "No way," I say and I close the door.

An Unsettling Dream

Mist hanging in the dew-drenched morning air. Mist hanging in the dew-drenched morning air, low fog as if all the lawns here had been seeded with dry ice. Mist hanging, low fog and a gray sky above as he appears. Jimmy, dressed in kenshi, the ceremonial vestments of a Kendo master, standing defiantly on that hallowed ground where his *foy-yay* would have been had I signed that variance, left foot back, weed whacker low at his side. In a show of strength, he has mobilized his Whirl-e-Gigs and other combative lawn ornaments, turned his in-ground sprinkler system on full ptyalize. In the distance I see the first regiment of infantry approach—a battalion of fruit-shaped realtors in diaphanous floral print blouses—the syncopated *thut-thut, thut-thut* of combat boots and steady cadence of FOY-YAY foofaraw, FOY-YAY foofaraw forces me to take cover behind a large azalea bush on our front lawn. They are supported by a division of Good Humor Ice Cream jeeps commandeered by disgruntled former students of mine in crisp dress whites. There is a chinkling of bells as the jeeps take up position a mere moment before the skies rain down that first sortie, Bomb Pops and Whammy Bars, Choco-Bursts and Toasted Almonds. The only other sound is the gut-numbing whir of that weed whacker, the horrific sound of filament severing the heads off of dandelions and baby blades of grass.

I awake with a shudder, my pillow moist with sweat, sheets in a tangle, my wife sitting up in bed beside me. "Bad dream?" she asks. "Yes," I say. "You OK now?" "Yes," I say. And as I fall slowly back into the aftermath of this dream, she begins to hum an aria from Bizet's *Carmen*. Soft. Seductive. *Habanera*. Her voice slowly descends as she runs a hand across my thigh and I know what the expectation is, but I cannot bring myself to face her, to embrace what this simple overture is calling for. "Not tonight," I say, "I'm sorry."

She pauses for a moment. "Daijobu," she whispers as she removes her hand, "Eee daijobu" (Japanese for *fine, perfectly fine*).

Up From His Dream of Eden, Rockwell Paints Cranford, NJ 07016

There is a clock that stands in the center of Cranford, N.J. 07016. And on Friday mornings at precisely 10:17 old men flock to it. Old men in cloth tams, their hair and beard stubble the color of chimney ash. They don't seem to mind that the clock has been frozen at 10:17 for years. Old men. They arrive as if by instinct. Relentless. True. Picture the swallows returning to Capistrano every March. Now picture something a bit less awe-inspiring. Downtown proper. 07016. A clock that is incapable or unwilling to move on. Old men perched on wooden benches. Old hands pecking at the crisp morning air. Hands like fragile birds. Hands like liver spotted windpeckers.

I am here. Cranford, New Jersey 07016. They call this place the *Venice of New Jersey*. Sort of poetic, I think. Idyllic even. When the moon sifts through the branches of Old Peppy (North America's largest deciduous Pepperidge Tree) I walk through town alone. I pass the movie theater and diner, and sometimes stop to stare at my reflection in the window of *Fuchsia, Forsythia, Gipani and Fink—Divorce Filings and Mediation A Specialty—Spouse's Signature Not Required*. Sometimes I find myself leaning on the wrought iron rail listening to the Rahway River as it trembles beneath the bridges on Eastman Street. Sometimes when the street lamps cast soft shadows on the pavement I sit with the empty benches and stare at that clock. 10:17 precisely. I swear I hear the sound of wings clapping in the night air. Birds in flight. And something a bit less awe-inspiring. I am here and I'm not sure why I stay. Sometimes. A man incapable or unwilling to move on. Gravipause, 07016.

4.

Still Life With Blue Collar Heirloom.

Clean-shaven and just out of the shower, he sits at the kitchen table. Dishes piled in the sink. A Ford Philco clock-radio prominently displayed on the shelf above his wife's Jesus. DJ's voice pushed out of a 3-inch speaker falls about the room, calls for early morning rain. A little after 6:00 am. A young father of two, soon three, sitting at a kitchen table, caught between all he once knew and all that is waiting for him if he has the strength to push away.

But it's that blue collar heirloom that haunts him now. A clock radio purchased with S & H Green stamps—years of delicately separating and licking, pressing into books that they would redeem. One day.

He sits alone at the table, studies cigarette burns: two perfect cockroaches etched into the surface, indelible testimony to another in a series of drunken nights. The apartment is still. The coffee is bitter and strong. He moves his cup two imaginary squares up, one over diagonally. Two up one over, as if it is some rogue knight and this whole thing is nothing more than a game. He is thinking about his sons, safe asleep, in their Hide-A-Bed upstairs. He is thinking about Madeline and the last time they made love. He is thinking about a conversation he had with his wife a few weeks back.

"I just can't believe it," she said, "Bobby Darin and Sandra Dee..."

"Hey, whaddya gonna do?"

"Guess that's what happens when you get rich and famous."

"That's why I've avoided it all these years."

"Silly. Promise me that you'll never pull a stunt like that."

"Believe me, you never have to sweat hearing about us on the radio."

"Kiss me."

He gets up to pour another cup of coffee as the DJ sends one out, this time to "all the cuties who work the luncheon counter at Woolworth's... A Wayne Newton POWERHIT."

Wayne Newton singing, "Danke schoen."

A Ford-Philco clock radio, blue-collar heirloom, flanked by a formation of his oldest son's plastic green army men.

And Wayne Newton singing.

He's thinking about his boys, and Sandra Dee, and Reno, and wondering if the Rambler will make it. Wondering how much he could get for that radio.

And more "Danke schoen". . .

Thinking about the night his wife wrested a bottle of 4 Roses from him and hid it in the pantry behind boxes of tapioca pudding, and the hangovers that kept him company on those mornings when she refused to speak to him. How he hated that silence. And how he hates tapioca pudding.

And, "Danke schoen". . .

He is thinking about Madeline.

Newton singing, "Danke schoen". . .

Thinking that she is probably teasing her hair up the way she does.

A packed valise hidden beneath the bed. Framed photograph on the nightstand—her husband and 13-year-old son in a canoe. Summer of '64.

And Wayne Newton singing. "Danke schoen". . .

He pushes away from the kitchen table.

Heads for the stairs.

Leaves the radio.

"Darling, Danke schoen". . .

On.

A Libretto for Pulsars

January 10, 2009: In a recent press release scientists at NASA indicated that they have detected sound in deep space. According to Dr. Alan Kogut from the Goddard Space Center, "The universe really threw us a curve. Instead of the faint signal we hoped to find, here was a booming noise six times louder than anyone had predicted." They claim that the origin of this "cosmic radio background" is still a mystery and that it defies the long held belief that there is no sound in outer space.

Meanwhile, in another part of the galaxy Elk are bugling just north of Boulder, Colorado. A night watchman snores in a high back swivel chair. Ex-con, with a five inch gutter-spike, scratches his name on the eastside stanchion of the Brooklyn Bridge. Two kids giggle into Dixie cup phones. 14 year old daughter of a West Nashville Deb moans into a Motel 6 pillow. And my mother, dressed in an island print muumuu softly hums the theme from *The Love Boat*. She is riding the bus from Bayonne to Atlantic City. Sitting by herself, counting her quarters. Dreaming of white sand beaches and rum drinks served in the hard, brown shell of a coconut, while a dark-skinned cabana boy fans her with a large palm frond.

⊕ *to CODA, Page 87*

Another Unsettling Dream

In this one I find myself shelved between the bookend likenesses of Bo Derek and Bo Diddley. Terrified. I call my buddy, BJ Ward, who is an Associate Specialist in Psychiatry at the Menninger Clinic. Actually, Ward was a patient at the Menninger Clinic but that was many years ago. He's much better now. He writes poetry and sells plumbing supplies in a place as vast and celebrated as Clute, Texas. Clute, as you may well know is where archeologists found the fossilized remains of a Mammoth named Asiel. There is a restaurant/museum in Clute built to commemorate this discovery. I believe it was reviewed by Zagat.

"Nothing to be concerned about," Ward tells me.

"Oh?"

"Yes, he says. "Sounds like "a touch of Generalized Anxiety Disorder tinged with traces of Sleep Apnea and Gender Identity Disorder—GID," he says.

"GID," I say.

"Make sure you get enough sleep—at least seven hours. Stay away from all dairy products and glutens. And by the way, are you getting laid much these days?"

"Define *much*..."

"Well then, there you are."

Allison

Now I ask you are there any words in this vast and expanding universe that sing more earthy, more libidinous, more inspiring, than "My husband has the kids this weekend."

5.

Flight of Stairs. Stairs are ambivalent. Leading up or leading out. A flight of stairs. A flight from memory. 6:19 am. He stands at the curtail, the soft, polished oak of finial beneath his hand. He is looking up a flight of stairs. Riser tread. Riser tread. A second floor landing and a closed door. He is heading up to kiss his sons, and whisper a soft goodbye and say a prayer but wonders for whom—a father leaving or for the sons he is leaving behind? As he takes the first step, he begins to think back...

Ascend

Tread.
Riser.

Tread.
Riser.

Tread.
Riser.

 Sitting on the stoop of some random Bergen Avenue tenement with his son, he takes a long pull from a pint in a brown paper bag. Fat man in a sweat stained tee shirt, suspenders and porkpie hat idles up.
 "What'd you have?" he asks.

"You know damn well what I had... 232."

Man in the pork pie pulls a roll of bills from his pocket, peels a few off. "Guess even a blind chicken gets a kernel once in a while," *he says as he hands over the money and continues up the block.*

"Who was that, dad?" his son asks.

"Nobody," he says and he hands the boy a crisp dollar bill, "for the candy store." He takes another swig from the bottle in the bag, brushes his son's hair back, "Don't tell your mother."

The boy smiles. Runs off.

Ascend

Tread.
Riser.

Tread.
Riser.

Sunday. May 9, 1966. Mother's Day. He is casing the Holy Name Cemetery. Early morning going from grave to grave filching flowers of all shapes and colors until he has a bouquet of some size. A sedan idles by. He ducks behind a mausoleum. The bells at Saint Aloysius begin their orotund yawning—mass is over, go in peace. He races out of the cemetery, beats her back to their small apartment just in time to place the flowers in a large mayonnaise jar, a makeshift vase. "Happy Mother's Day!"

Ascend

Tread.
Riser.

Tread.
Riser.

Jobs that he could not hold over the years as if one can actually hold a job the way one holds a pocket watch heirloom or a child's hand. Just out of the service, he works as a janitor at Hellman's Real Mayonnaise. A Fuller Brush salesman. Postal clerk. Soda jerk. Day laborer. Night watchman. Bell hop. Grease monkey. Car jockey. Milkman. Bag man. Bartender. Gravedigger. And each time he quits, is fired, or swears he has a line on something a bit more promising they sit at the kitchen table, and have the same abrupt and fruitless exchange.

"When is this all gonna stop?" his wife asks, never looking him in the eye.

"Don't push," he says, "I'll work it out."

Ascend

Tread.
Riser.

Tread.
Riser.

An honorable discharge. Parris Island, South Carolina. The weight of a three year hitch off his back, he is headed home. High and tight. Swamp rat. United States Marine. She lures him off of his stool at the Depot Bar and Grille and leads him to a dimly lit back room. Blue-eyed Suzie. A local girl. "Five," she says as she undoes his belt and slides her hand beneath his khakis. Outside, a Greyhound wheezes as it pulls in, same bus that will take him back to Jersey in an hour or so, back to his young wife. Semper fi.

Ascend

Tread.
Riser.

Tread.
Riser.

A Lockheed Constellation. TWA flight 132 Newark to Miami. He stares out the cabin window as the plane cuts through a wisp of clouds, rises another step. He turns to his Ivory scrubbed bride then to the stewardess, orders his fourth scotch and soda. Prelude to a honeymoon.

  Ascend

                        Tread.
                    Riser.

                Tread.
            Riser.

He stands motionless on the second floor landing. A closed
door, and beyond that door his sons—two tiny engines soon to
emerge from sleep's dark tunnel. What will he say? And what will he
say that could possibly matter? A kiss on the forehead? Perhaps. He
pauses before reaching for the doorknob, stares the door down—a
fragile barrier that keeps him from love—the only engine strong
enough to deliver him, shunt him back to the life he knew before
Madeline. But he does not go in. No. He turns, places his hand on
the banister...

and

            Tread
                riser.

                    Tread
                        riser.

                        Tread.
                            riser.

                                Slowly descends.

Suite Infidelity

The Planets, Opus 32 *was first performed with the London Symphony Orchestra on November 15, 1920. Composer Gustav Holst endeavored to capture the astrological resonance of each of the seven observable planets in our solar system in the seven movements of this orchestral suite.*

First Movement — A Letter from Cheryl

Briney,

It's taken longer than I expected. Many a detour—deported in Amsterdam, arrested in New Orleans, but I've finally made it back, back over the asylum wall and I must say Cayo Huesa has never looked more deliciously decadent. I'm presently holed up on houseboat row with my Chihuahua Uno (you remember, one nut) and a pet barracuda that swims up to my transom every morning, I feed him on slivers of Cuban toast and used condoms. Working at the Key West Natural Market across from Capt. Tony's—moving a whole shit pile of Inositol, go figure. At night I'm back singing at the Parrot and moving a different type of merchandise. And so it goes my confrere (now is the time that you should be seated and if possible mildly sedated) that I have given myself over to those appetites that you so ardently spoke of when last we were together over cups in Boulder, CO. And I must admit that it pains me to tell you this, but I am in love again, and this time it's a man. He's married but spiritual, drinks too much and is heavily into reiki and daily high colonics. I met him at a lesbian tea (don't ask) and in no short time found myself completely smitten with him. And Briney, me old scout—I can see you shaking your head like you always did when I, nose packed with dumb dust, tried to convince you that I kicked. "Ah, Cheryl... no, no, no." And I guess I deserved it, and must tell you that I have my doubts but I think it is love, deep unendurable love, or maybe it's just the sex. Whatever it is, if I can survive it this time without a drool bucket and protective custody it will be a major boon to lovers worldwide. Be happy for me, my friend, but leave the training wheels on. And just one more thing—there's rumor down here that against all odds and expectations you are *still* married. Is this true? What is it that Japanese women have that we, on this side of the marble, seem to have overlooked?

Keeping an eye on the night sea, awaiting your arrival,
Cheryl

Second Movement — Viagra

I lost my dick. Of all the things to lose in the course of a lifetime—car keys, cuff links, phone numbers scribbled on bar napkins, dead grandmother's recipe for Manhattan clam chowder—I lost my dick. I'm not quite sure how this happened. I mean, I just reached down one morning and it was gone. AWOL. Remember GI Joes? At least they had guns...

My dick bears an uncanny resemblance to the actor Mickey Rourke. Think of *Body Heat* or *9 1/2 Weeks* or *The Pope of Greenwich Village.* At first, I wanted to tell my wife, but then thought better of it—she doesn't do well with this type of thing. I remember once I misplaced several swatches of cloth that we were considering for window treatments. When I told her what I'd done she scaled the rail of our deck and with arms outstretched threatened to throw herself headlong into the sea of leaves that was our backyard—threatened to throw herself, not unlike the Japanese war widows who, rather than risk dishonor, hurled themselves from the Cliffs of Sandempeki into the hungry Pacific. No, I would not be telling my wife.

Weeks pass and I do all those things you might expect of one who has lost his dick. I contact the local authorities, check milk cartons, make hand drawn fliers that offer a modest reward and nail them to every lamp post in the neighborhood. I search those places where all dicks go when they've gone soft, get desperate, or feel under-appreciated: Balcony at the Orpheus, back room of Good Vibrations Adult Books and Erotic Oddments, lingerie department at Delilah's, bathroom stall in the men's room at the Cranford train station, but I come up empty.

One night while running an errand for my wife I happen upon a figure slumped against a Salvation Army drop box in the back parking lot of Barnett's Pharmacy. He looks strung out, familiar, flaccid. Staggers up to my car. "You got any V? Just a taste, baby, just a taste..." and I know at a glance it's my very own quim tickler. Cycloptic milk-spitter. My twenty first digit. Get in I say and we pull out slowly. Me, feeling enmity, relief. My dick jonesing for a hit of Viagra. "C'mon baby, just a taste of V, one hit..." he begs, a desperate Mickey Rourke, think of *Barfly* or *The Wrestler*. I glance over, but already know what needs to be done. We ride home in silence, save for the ambient sounds of the night, a man and his prodigal member.

Third Movement — My Wife Takes Lovers

"She plays the pee-ann-ah," he says.

"Plays the *pee-ann-ah?*" I say, "My wife takes lovers..."

It was a Chickering Traditional Baby Grand. 1933. Fully restored. A gift for my wife on our third wedding anniversary. The guys who delivered it looked as if they had been sculpted from the sidewalks of Brooklyn. "Where do you want we should put it?" said the one with the goat's head tattoo and Pall Mall cigarette tucked behind one ear. "Over there," I said, "in the corner." And with as much effort as a child would expend lifting an empty box of crayons they raised then positioned the *pee-ann-ah* in the one sunlit corner of our living room. I signed the requisite papers, pink copy, yellow copy, and they were on their way.

In truth, I knew of my wife's passion for big pianists and her proclivity for classical composition long before the arrival of that dulcet Trojan Horse. What I did not know then, nor fully understand now is how that *pee-ann-ah*—1933 Chickering fully restored— would infiltrate, seduce, and appropriate my wife's affections.

It all started quite innocently, as most trysts do. *Adagietto.* Husband lying on the couch watching *Get Smart* re-runs. Sunday afternoons. Wife in the next room running scales, delicate trills that lead to soft arpeggios. At first, innocent flirtations. *Preludes* and *Etudes.*

Chopin, Schumann, Schubert.

But I should have seen it coming, should have been more attentive, I guess, but ain't that the way it goes. I mean we fall in love, then begin to take love for granted, get all too comfortable— nights of hot, wet, sex replaced by trips to HOME DEPOT to purchase crown molding and patio furniture—then after a stubborn emotional silence we find ourselves more or less alone and ask "What on Earth went wrong?" *Poco a poco.* I'm in bed, while my wife is downstairs, dressed in one of my old Levi work shirts and nothing else. She's caressing keys.

Beethoven, Mendelssohn, Bach.

Here are some words I looked up one afternoon at the Cranford Public Library. I found them in a book titled *Musical Terms All Piano Players Should Know.* I pored over that book with the same careful attention that some men reserve for road maps and instruction manuals. Don't ask me why.

Polyphonic Music—*Any musical composition in which two or more melodies are heard simultaneously.*

Capo—*Head or The beginning of a Movement or musical*

composition.

Accarezzévole—*Expressive, caressing.*

Dolce—*Sweetly, softly.*

Lento—*Slowly.*

Legato—*Smoothly.*

Vibrato—*Vary the pitch with rapid movement of the left hand.*

Moderato—*Gradually increase tempo.*

Grazioso—*Gracefully*

Improvisando—*Improvise*

Segue—*Go on with what follows.*

Presto—*Accelerate. Quickly.*

Forte—*Loud.*

Prestissimo—*Rapid, as fast as possible.*

Crescendo—*Grow gradually louder, stronger.*

Tenuto- *Sustain.*

Fortissimo- *Very loud, powerful.*

Sforzando—*Explosively.*

Ritardando—*Gradually slow down.*

Fermata—*A pause.*

Tacet—*Be silent.*

Fine—*End.*

Da Capo Al Fine—*Return to the beginning and play to the word "fine" once more.*

"She plays the pee-ann-ah," the man said some years ago.

"Plays the pee-ann-ah," I say. "My wife's a whore for Prokofiev!"

And it only gets worse, *Fantasy in C Major, Appasionata, Goldberg Variations*—she's in there right now with her men, men with names like Serge, Maurice, Johannes, Franz, Frederic, Edvard and Wolfgang. She plays them. And they fill her, fill her in ways that I could never. Debussy splayed across the piano desk. Sheet music strewn about the floor. Slender fingers kissing keys. She's leaning in. Opening herself up. What more can I do than sequester myself away in the next room—cuckold in a Lazy Boy, and listen as they take my wife.

Mozart, Ravel, Stravinsky.

My wife is having affairs and there is very little that I can do about it. My wife is having affairs and there is very little that I can do. My wife is having affairs *Fine.*

Fourth Movement — Heavenly Bodies

Standing below a cut of trees in our backyard, combing the night sky with my Meade 14 Advanced Ritchey-Chrétien Telescope (Observatory clarity—for the serious astronomer), I'm trying to find the Asterisms of Ursa Major and Ursa Minor when my sight line is interrupted by something wholly unexpected. She's standing naked, framed by the second floor bathroom window, Jimmy's wife Jamie. She is toweling herself off, unaware that the blind slats lie flat on their backs affording any neighborhood kid or serious astronomer a nearly unobstructed view of her firm breasts, perfect pudendum and fleur-de-lis wall paper. And I think, for a moment, that I really should look away, retire the telescope and call it a night, but then with a tug of the draw string she raises the idle blinds, and taps on the window with a long, red fingernail (actually the color was *vermilion vixen*. I only know this because she volunteered this one day having just returned from a *mani-pedi*—her word—at some day spa while Jimmy was out of town on Good Humor business). She doesn't hesitate, doesn't undulate, bump, grind, fondle, grope, probe, or caress—no—she merely stares at her naked reflection in the window, both of us gazing at that heavenly body for some time and then Jamie, Jimmy's loving wife of 14 years, treasurer of the local Junior League, slides a vermilion vixen into her mouth, runs it across her lips and mouths just one word... *pulchritude...* her lips pursed and then slowly closing around me with... *pulchritude.*

Fifth Movement — The Allison Affair

Allison and I have been having an affair for the last three years. I'm not proud of that fact. I'm not ashamed of it, either. We were having breakfast. Black bean frittatas, fresh cantaloupe, and homemade biscuits. Sitting at the island, granite top surrounded by her recently remodeled kitchen, while her two sons were off with her x-husband for the weekend. This is what the court order called for. So, this is what he does. His name is Ronnie. He's a deputy sheriff in Alpha. Allison says that Ronnie is a good father to his boys. On Saturdays when it's *his weekend* he likes to take them to the movies and sometimes to the Pequest Trap and Skeet Club. This is the conversation that Allison and I had one morning while eating black

68

bean frittatas on an island in her kitchen while her x-husband and two sons were off shooting clay pigeons at a range in Pequest.

"No," I say, "I just don't see it that way."

"It's still fucking around," she says.

"I don't get you. I mean, if they just meet for coffee, or dinner, or whatever—a walk in the park and just talk—no sex, just talk…"

"It's still fucking around."

"If they're just talking?"

"Well it depends."

"Depends on *what*?

"What they're talking about."

Allison taps a jar of salsa with her spoon, then tries to pry it open with the flat end. She reaches across the island, hands me the jar. I open it. She smiles.

"Can I ask you something," she says.

"Sure," I say.

"If you and I were not doing to each other what we did to each other last night, but were still getting together for breakfast, talking—what would you call *that?*"

"I don't know… having breakfast… talking."

"Really?"

"I guess."

Her cell phone rings. She motions for me to be quiet. I go to the refrigerator, find a carton of OJ, take a swig, and put it back on the shelf. Allison stares into her coffee mug. She looks tired, bored, angry. I've seen her like this at work, usually when a drunk short tips her or a regular asks a really stupid question. We answer a lot of really stupid questions at Frankie Shine's Candlelight Inn, but I guess that's just part of the job.

"Can I ask you something else?" she says without looking up from the mug.

"That depends," I say.

"Do you have these conversations with your wife?"

"What conversations?"

"You know, like we do—"

"No, hell no—"

"Why not?"

"I don't know. I really don't think she'd be that interested."

"No?"

"No."

"Then what do you two talk about?"

"Nothing really, I guess. Why the sudden interest in my wife?"

Allison doesn't respond.

I don't press.

A few minutes drift by.

"So, you really don't think it's fucking around," she says.

"We've been over this already," I say.

"Even if they share their most intimate personal secrets?"

"Are they naked when they're sharing these secrets?"

"You're impossible," she says and she throws a biscuit at me. It hits me directly in the forehead.

"You got any fresh-chopped cilantro?" I ask. "This would be better with some cilantro..."

"Impossible," she says.

I nod as I reach for the last slab of cantaloupe. "Cilantro?"

Sixth Movement — Making Crepe

1 Cup All-Purpose Flour

1 tsp. White Sugar

¼ tsp. salt

3 large eggs

2 cups heavy cream

2 tbsp. ghee (clarified butter)

Sift together flour, sugar, salt-set aside. Whisk eggs and heavy cream together. Combine with flour mixture. Add ghee and stir until smooth.

Heat a lightly oiled crepe pan over medium heat. Spoon in batter, approximately 2 tbsp. for each crepe. Tip pan slightly and move in a circular motion to spread batter as thinly as possible. Turn crepe until both sides are golden brown. Serve hot with fruit or crème filling.

How the world loves crepe! Delicate. Enticing. Filled with fresh strawberries, dusted with powdered sugar. Sweet crêpe. Dessert crêpe. Crêpe Marron. Crêpe Suzette. Crêpe Susanne. Crepe Pam, Crepe Doris, Chloe, Rachel, Crepe Vanessa the hedonic hairdresser. Crêpe A La Mousse Au Chocolat. Crêpe A La Missionary. Just can't get enough. Crepe for breakfast. Crepe for lunch. Late night crepe folded in designer sheets. And there's more. Much more. Eating crepe while reading Miller's *Sexus*. Crepe on the Board Room conference table. Crepe during the rain delay of the Yankees-Boston matinee. Sticky, sweat-drizzled crepe. Oo-La-La. Ask the young second lieutenant what he will miss most after he is deployed and he will tell you, "The hot, golden skin of crepe pressed softly to my lips. Crepe La Banane.

Crepe Au Fromage. Crepe garnished with the pubic hair of silent film sirens. Crepe Garbo. Crepe Pickford. Crepe Goddard. Ah, how we all do adore crepe. Hot house crepe. Tantalizing tantric crepe. Crepe that fills your nostrils with the distinct odor of Barnegat Bay at low tide. Crepe that whirs and vibrates, eaten while you're bound and lovingly spanked. A meal to be savored. A meal to be shared. Ménage à crepe...

Seventh Movement — *The Star Ledger*

"Come Fly With Me"—The lead story in the Sunday Newark *Star Ledger* heralded the exploits of Steve Fossett, American millionaire, aviator, adventurer. Fossett, in his Virgin Atlantic Global Flyer, completed the first non-stop, non-refueled flight around the world. According to the *Ledger*, the trip took 67 hours, 1 minute at an average speed of 342.2 mph.

Other headlines included: *Tulip Revolution Flowers—Akayev Ousted*, and *Camden Wife Throws Husband's Prosthetic Leg in Shark Tank*.

Also in the news:

> Married Couple Makes Out On Couch
> A forty-six-year-old bartender and his wife of eleven years confirmed reports that they did make out on their living room sofa last Thursday night. The husband, who also works as an adjunct professor of astronomy at Wood Hills Community College, delivered the following from the couple's front porch:
> "First, I want to thank you all for coming out. I

will read a prepared statement and then answer no questions. With regard to the alleged making out that occurred at this residence, Thursday, March 1, 2005: I did, in fact, tongue kiss my wife of eleven years, Sadako (née Okada) Bradford, kissing her repeatedly about the mouth and neck. This act was unprovoked and not, in any way, premeditated. Candidly, it came as quite a surprise to us both. I know that many, especially those who are among the legion of the long-married will find this act inconceivably rash, even a bit disgusting, but it happened and we make no apologies—public or private."

Bradford did comment in a follow-up interview with the Ledger that, "the kissing did not lead to intercourse," but he was not "ruling that out" in the future. His wife was unavailable for comment.

"Hanashitai koto ga arundakedo."

6.

The Letter. Odd, what he thought of when he first sat down to write it—how the Sisters at Saint Aloysius always went out of their way to compliment him on what beautiful penmanship he had.

> To my Wife and Sons,

Too impersonal.

> Dearest Margaret and Sons

Liar.

> Maggie,

Too soft. Too much history.

> Margaret,

It'll have to do.

> Margaret,
> There is nothing that I can do at this point that will make this easier for you, so I'll just come right out and say it— I'm leaving, and I'm not coming back. I know you must

think I'm the biggest coward that has ever lived and you probably hate me—god knows you have the right, but I just feel... just feel... I feel...

Tell her.

> Margaret,
> First, let me say that I am so ashamed and sorry for what I am doing and if there was any other way I could make this work for all of us I would. But I know I have to go. And I know I won't be coming back. The pain I feel in my heart at this moment, knowing that I will never see you or the boys again...

"Ashamed and sorry... pain I feel in my heart." Oh please, you don't mean a word of that. Tell her. You owe her at least that much.

> Margaret,
> When you read this, I know your first thought will be to try and find me. Probably call work, Ruther's, my mother, please don't as they have absolutely no idea of what I'm about to say. I'm leaving. I know that of all the cruel things that a man could do, leaving his two young sons and pregnant wife is something that deserves the deepest, darkest hell as punishment. But I also know that if I don't do this I will bring that hell down on you, the boys, and our unborn child...

Sooner or later she is going to find out.

> Margaret,
> Let me start by assuring you that there is not now, nor has there ever been another woman. Having said that, let me get right to the point—I'm not sure what's gone wrong, maybe it's guilt, the guilt

> I feel for having constantly failed you, or maybe I'm just not cut out for this kind of life, I don't know... maybe it's boredom, What I mean is and this is so damn hard to say—I just don't think we're going to make it.

Stop mincing words. For once, just say it—tell her the truth.

> Margaret,
> I know that what I've done will bring hard times for you and the boys, but I also know that you will all be better off in the long run. Who knows why people do what they do. Margaret, you always said you were a survivor (remember the unsinkable Molly Brown) and this is one of the few things I guess we both agreed on over the years. Somewhere down the road, I know you will let go of the anger and sense of betrayal that you must be feeling right now. Maybe you'll even come to understand that there was really nobody to blame here...

What's stopping you? Why can't you just come out with it? Actually, she's as much to blame as you are. Sure, you made your mistakes but wasn't she always right there, every step of the way, to remind you of them all in full measure...

"You drink too much."

"You smoke too much."

"Can't save a dime."

"Shutting the electric off on Monday."

"I'm pregnant."

"I'm pregnant."

"I'm pregnant."

Margaret,

For chrissake! She'll get over it eventually. You'll send money. The boys will be fine; in time they will forget about you, or maybe forgive you, maybe even come out to visit one day.

Margaret...

Look at the clock. They'll be getting up soon.

> Margaret,
> There is no other way to say this. I have fallen in love with another woman. Don't ask me to make sense of this whole damn mess. I have no answers for you. I guess it's just one of those things, ya know.

A letter to his wife. Left on the kitchen table. October, 22, 1966. A little after 6:40 in the a.m.

Rabbit in the Moon

Rabbit in the Moon: Based in Japanese folklore, the Rabbit in the Moon or Jade rabbit is the Eastern counterpart of Western culture's Man in the Moon. According to Japanese myth, moon markings depict the form of a rabbit with a mortar and pestle. It is believed that the rabbit is pounding ingredients to make mochi, an Asian staple and traditional food used to celebrate the Japanese New Year (from a list entitled Full-Moon Names and Their Meanings—Celestial Folklore/ Mythology Almanac).

My wife and I write notes these days. Notes affixed to the refrigerator door. Hastily written asides set in the margins of an eleven-year marriage. And did I mention that our refrigerator door is avocado green, same color as a leisure suit that I once wore, but that was a long time ago. 1976. I believe. Back when disco was all the rage. And I admit, this unnerves me at times, I mean, our refrigerator door. There are times I wish we would curbside it, replace it with something a little more 21st century. French door. Ice dispenser. Stainless steel would be nice. The thing is, whenever I bring this up with my wife, I get to feeling sentimental, even a bit guilty. My friend, the poet BJ Ward says it's because I'm a Catholic (which he pronounces *Cat-Lick*). "Why don't you get rid of that damn thing," he says as he casts a disdainful eye at our refrigerator.

"Can't do it," I say, "too much history."

Ward rubs his chin and nods, "Cat-Licks," he says with a smirk.

What Ward can't seem to see is that the refrigerator in all its avocado ugliness has taken on great spiritual significance in our marriage, has become a Mecca of sorts, a place where daily lamentations and grocery lists are reverently posted. Think of the Wailing Wall. Now think of the Wailing Wall awash in gangrenous green paint, prayers affixed across the whole expanse with round smiley-face-have-a-nice-day kitchen magnets. Get the picture? *Usagi usagi... Nani mite haneru... Jugoya o-tsuki-sama... Mite haneru... Usagi usagi... Nani mite haneru... Jugoya o Usagi usagi... Nani mite haneru... Jugoya o-tsuki-sama... Mite haneru... *

Here is a note that my wife left on our refrigerator door just this afternoon, right before she went off to attend Jugoya with Michiko, an old friend visiting from Osaka:

> Husband,
>   This weekend I go to New York for shiatsu and then to Jugoya with Michiko-san. Please remember to pick up milk and Panko for Monday tonkatsu.
>   Don't forget to go to gym. You are a little bit losing your cool stuff these days. I am decidedly worry insofar as your health. I am worry insofar as your low energy. Don't forget the Panko.
>
> Your Wife

traditional song, sung at harvest celebrations and the full moon festival

I have folded myself into the lotus position—a sound not unlike granola crunching beneath my skin. Note in my lap as I sit facing the refrigerator. I begin to meditate. It takes me back to when it was just the two of us. My wife and I.

Usagi usagi... Nani mite haneru... Jugoya o-tsuki-sama... Mite haneru... Usagi usagi... Nani mite haneru... Jugoya o Usagi usagi... Nani mite haneru... Jugoya o-tsuki-sama... Mite haneru...

I see us huddled in the tall grass—a field in Kyoto as the full moon throws light on Anao-Ji the 21rst temple in the Saigoku pilgrimage. Jugoya, 1992.

"Look," I say as I point to the night sky, "it's the Man in the Moon."

"*Rabbit* in the Moon," she says.

"Rabbit?" I say. "Why say rabbit?"

"It *is* Rabbit."

"What is he doing up there?"

"Making mochi, of course, for tonight's Jugoya."

"Of course," I say.

Usagi usagi... Nani mite haneru... Jugoya o-tsuki-sama... Mite haneru... Usagi usagi... Nani mite haneru... Jugoya o Usagi usagi... Nani mite haneru... Jugoya o-tsuki-sama... Mite haneru...

Meditation over and back from the gym. And shopping. And Frankie's. I put the groceries down on the kitchen table, next to the note. The room is dark and I'm a little bit drunk and feeling sorry for myself. You see, *I have lost my cool stuff.* I'm not quite sure when that happened. But I don't doubt it. My wife is off with Michiko, singing traditional Japanese songs, no doubt, eating mochi and using words like *decidedly* and *insofar as*— this from a woman who has taken to English like a Vegan takes to Mulligan Stew. And I wonder where she picked that up. And wonder why it should really matter. It doesn't. But I do miss her when she's not around sometimes. Miss her even more when she is sitting directly across from me. Sometimes.

Usagi usagi... Nani mite haneru... Jugoya o-tsuki-sama... Mite haneru... Usagi usagi... Nani mite haneru... Jugoya o Usagi usagi... Nani mite haneru... Jugoya o-tsuki-sama... Mite haneru...

Standing on our back deck now, staring up at the full moon, and the rabbit who is still working away, pounding rice with his mallet, making mochi for this year's Jugoya, I can't help but wonder what keeps him there, what keeps her here, and think about Kyoto—if the moon still casts a soft glow on Anoa Ji and on the tall grass where we once sat holding hands.

"Hanashitai koto ga arundakedo."

"..."

7.

Flight of Stairs. He peers down another stairwell. Smirks at the darkness he has brought on, a light bulb that he promised to replace weeks ago, like so many other things here that he just never got around to doing. A red sweater draped across his arm, road map in his pocket. He has no suitcase, no time for second thoughts. A narrow passage. Sad avenue of steps descending.

Tread
    Riser
        Tread
            Riser
                Tread
                    Riser
                        FIRST FLOOR LANDING

Alone in the vestibule. One final door stands between where he is going and what he is leaving behind. He pauses for a moment before silently sliding the chain lock. The last stern line tossed, he is a small craft in the darkness, adrift between pylons, unencumbered, heading out.

Exploring the Pleiades

One of the closest open star clusters to Earth, The Pleiades (Messier 45) is located in the constellation of Taurus. According to Greek mythology the seven brightest stars in this cluster represent the seven daughters of Atlas who were cast into the night sky to spare them from Orion's pursuit.

The planetarium at Wood Hills Community College is one of the only air-conditioned buildings on campus. It has a Zeiss Model M1015 star projector, MC10 state of the art Media Control Center with a 2000 watt Dolby Surround Sound system, all gifts from the estate of the late Dr. C.P. Cosworth, professor emeritus. There is a portrait of Cosworth in the planetarium lobby. He bears an uncanny resemblance to the singer Buddy Holly only not as buff, and is wearing a herring bone tweed jacket and holding a pipe. He looks very confused.

The planetarium was built in 1968 and refurbished in 2007. Above the entrance the words *Cosmic Inspiring Eternal* are etched in a bronze-plated plaque. There are many alcoves and secluded nooks here. I'm here, too. Every Tuesday and Thursday night. 6:00 to 9:50. I'm one of four assistant directors of the planetarium, and an adjunct professor at Wood Hills. Tonight I'm doing a lesson on the Pleiades.

Astronomy 155 Section A. It's odd, but whenever I teach this lesson my mind wanders to Tennessee Williams. I think of a moment in *A Streetcar Named Desire* when Blanche Dubois is flirting with Mitch. "I'm looking for the Pleiades," she says in her coquettish Southernese, "the seven sisters, but these girls are not out tonight. Oh yes, there they are, there they are! God Bless them! All in a bunch going home from their little bridge party." Mitch nods, tries to kiss her. Five minutes before class begins.

Astronomy 155

Students file in through the *Cosmic Inspiring Eternal* portal. They find their seats as I gradually bring down the lights and illuminate the hemispheric dome. Quiet for a moment. And then my voice, resonant, low-slung FM groove, fills the galaxy that is the Woodland Hills Community College Planetarium:

> We are traveling tonight to one of the most prominent galactic formations in our solar system. The Pleiades. Roughly 135 parsecs (440 light years) from earth. The first step in what's known as the cosmic ladder in our universe. Composed mostly of luminous, hot blue stars developed over the last 100 million years... easily sighted with the naked eye during the winter months in the northern hemisphere... summer months in the southern hemisphere... a chance alignment calculated at 1 in 500,000 relative motion... giant molecular clouds... reflection nebulae... estimated to exist for the next 250 million years...

An hour or so into the lesson and I have totally lost them—sent them adrift into a much deeper kind of space—they are floating, being pulled away by a force greater than gravity, the impelling power of boredom. Some head for the bathroom or out for a smoke, some explore the carnal possibilities afforded by those dark alcoves that I mentioned before—Gemini astronauts in search of something that truly is *Cosmic Inspiring Eternal*. And I, too, am light years away, my voice the only thing that tethers me to the moment. Adrift. I'm thinking about Allison. And Cheryl. And six and a half years of graduate school, a PHD, and *A Libretto For Pulsars*. I am thinking about Blanche Dubois, and old man Cosworth, Buddy Holly, and Mitch...

This completes our exploration of the Pleiades, my voice now heavy with the weight of a two-hour recitation, finds its way about the near empty room, *Are there any questions?*

When the last of the remaining students shuttle for the exits I close down the star projector and media center, pack up my Embassy Saddle Bag (luxurious genuine leather for those who trek the urban jungle with style), and head for the door.

Ursa Major

The night sky is uncharacteristically clear as I make my way across campus. Ursa Major is visible to the north. Directly opposite I can see the distinct W pattern of Cassiopeia and I think of Ptolemy and what he thought when he first came upon it. I wonder what his colleagues said, and if his wife waited up for him that night. Sometimes I wonder if there is anything still left, still unseen. Holly's Comet, perhaps. The Dubois Nebula. *Cosmic Inspiring Eternal.* I think about Ptolemy, wonder if he ever cheated on his wife. I wonder if he ever taught a section of Astronomy 155. Or if he could.

"Hanashitai koto ga arundakedo."

"Come again?"

8.

Rambler. The first thing he feels is the chill morning air like a rasp out of ice water dragged across his clean-shaven face. He pushes past the gate, hears the latch clack behind him, doesn't look back. The windshield of the Rambler is covered with a thin veil of frost, so he opens the car door, kneels, searches beneath the bench seat—two unpaid parking tickets, Help Wanted ads from the *Jersey Journal*, a small, blue, plastic shovel. He begins to scrape the windshield with the shovel, the frost comes off in rolls, falls on his bare knuckles like cold lace. Key in the ignition, the Rambler turns over after several attempts.

He sits on the curb, waits for the car to warm up, picks a Rheingold cap from the gutter—*My beer is Rheingold the dry beer. Think of Rheingold whenever you buy beer. It's not bitter, not sweet. It's the extra dry treat. Won't you buy, won't you try Rheingold beer—* runs his thumb over the bottle cap's scalloped edges as if it were a shell from some exotic island. Madeline. The heat from the engine warms him for a moment. And he feels the morning sun on his face.

The slow thaw of leaving. And starting over. And distance. Distance. With little left to do here, he rises, tosses the bottle cap into a storm drain, slides behind the wheel of the idling car, and pulls slowly away.

Birth of a Star

It begins in the spiral arms of galaxies. Nebulae, clouds of dust and hydrogen gas appear in these stellar incubators and, as a result of gravitational forces and extreme heat, tiny, rotating globules are formed. These amorphous masses then collapse as a result of shock waves emitted from supernovae. In time (10,000 to 1, 000,000 years) the rotation speed and temperature increases, forming a protoplanetary disc. The central core of this disk solidifies, resulting in the birth of a star.

One cold, clear night, some 100 light years away, a globule of gas and dust is slowly rotating just within the stellar nursery known as the Orion Nebula.

"Hanashitai koto ga arundakedo."
"Once more, please. Slowly."

As this globule or molecular cloud begins to rotate faster it contracts. As a result a protostar is formed. Its core reaching heat in excess of 15 million degrees centigrade.

"Hana—shi—tai—koto—ga—arunda—kedo."

"I see... *What* is it that you need to tell me?"

At this extremely high temperature hydrogen and helium gases begin to fuse. The mass stops contracting and emits energy causing it to shine.

"Bo ni ninshin shita."
"You what?"

As helium in the core is exhausted, an outer gaseous shell breaks away. This shell that surrounds the core is called a planetary nebula.

"Bo ni ninshin shita." She removes the empty box from her purse. *Clearblue Plus* (double confirmation of the results. Accuracy just got easier). "I pissed on stick."

"... AND?"

Over the course of the next one million years (average gestation period for stars) a series of nuclear reactions occurs, creating more shells around the core.

"Ko O yadoshite iru."

The core then collapses in a matter of seconds causing a violent explosion known as a supernova.

"WHAT..?"

"Ko O yadoshite iru—I'm preg-goo-nant."

The force emitted from the explosion that creates the supernova jettisons all outer shells.

"Preg-goo-nant?"

"Yes."

The remaining core (weighing 1.5 to 3.0 solar masses) results in the birth of a Neutron Star.

"Absolutely sure?"

"Sure."

One cold, clear night. A husband and wife. Worn wooden bench in an empty plaza. Clock frozen at 10:17.

"Really..."

She nods.

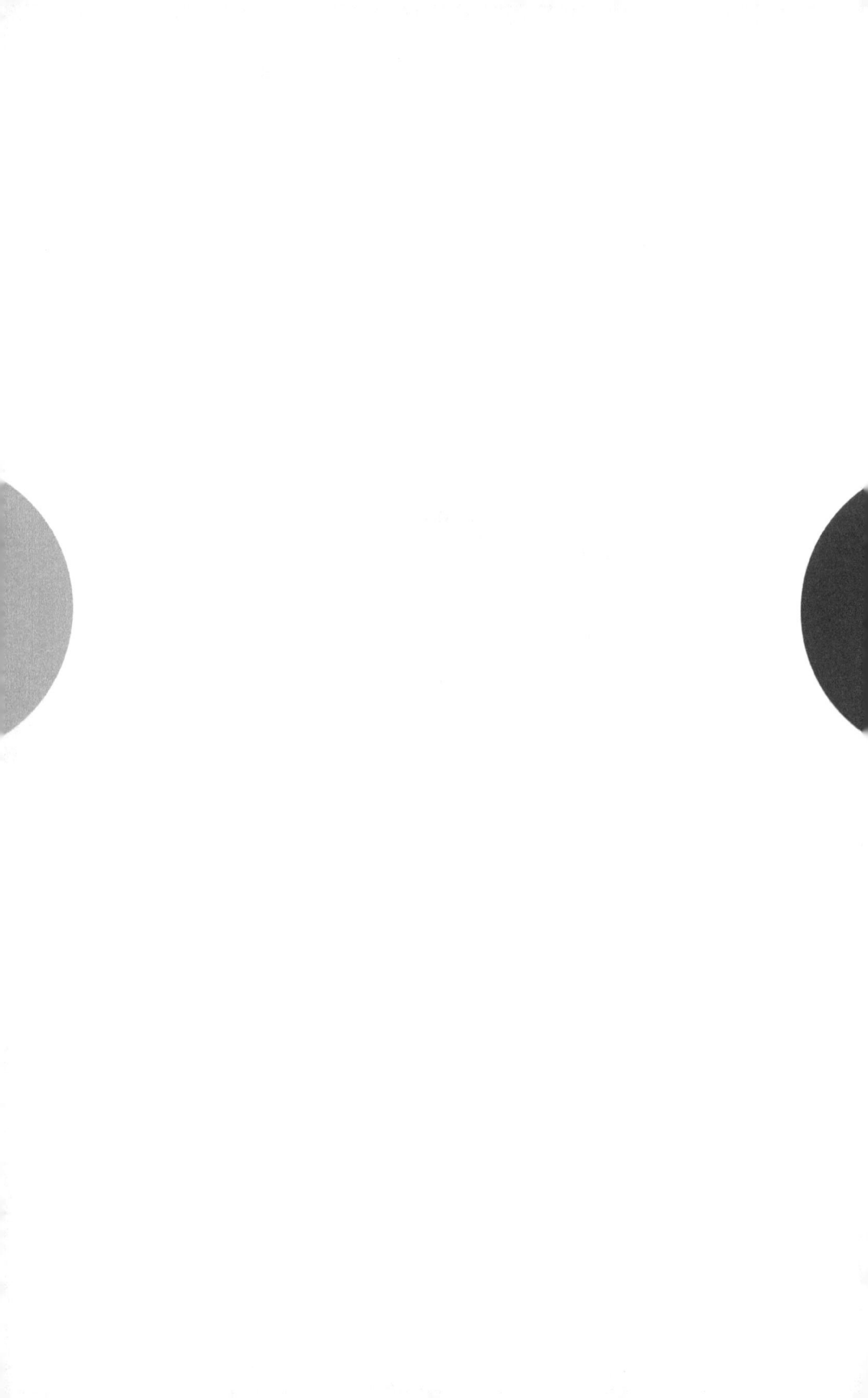

Defying Gravity

gravity (grav e tee) n. One of the four universal interactions in nature. The reciprocal pull or force of attraction between two masses. According to Newton's Law of Gravitation, F=mg. Where F represents the force of attraction, m-the object's mass, g-the acceleration due to gravity-this number is constant for all masses of matter.

Words are not bound by gravity. They free-float, trailing behind skywriters at the beach. Dancing in that empty space between lovers. A pas de deux. Words, free from gravity, but not weightless. And how can I make this clear to my wife as we find ourselves back at the kitchen table. Another Sunday morning. Me snorting lines of Carnation Instant Breakfast—Mocha Madness. My hair, in a manic slam dance, powdered chocolate residue highlighting my nostrils—I am Nosferatu's manservant. My wife, pregnant and pretty, is floating out names like tiny, delicate kites from a book of traditional Japanese monikers.

"If we have girl maybe Ayuko, means child of love. Or maybe Atsuko—warm child. Or how about Yukiko which means snow child or Hamako means child of the beach, or Hajime—new beginning..."

Hamako, Yukiko, Ayuko. Each name like a small bag of sand slowly dragging me down as I try to stay afloat, and feel the ghost hand of my father pushing me, his whiskey breath and cold stare, unsympathetic, mocking, forcing me under. I pull away from the table and swim out into the autumn air as my wife's words trail behind.

"If boy how about Hideharu means flourishing autumn or Hyousuke means helpful soldier or Hisashi... near always or Hitomu... one dream."

Outside, my neighbor Jimmie has convened the wise men in his drive way. He is humming *O Holy Night,* painting a plastic replica of Christ Jesus. Jimmie standing with ox and ass, a paint brush in his hand, peculiar smile on his face—the smile of a man who has just auditioned for a Mentos commercial.

"Just touching up the Son of Man," Jimmie's voice makes its pilgrimage across the yard.

I ignore him as I head for my hammock, a genuine Pawley Island rope job (a bit of island flair that you can take home with you). A moment and I am staring up at clouds, gently rocking, defying gravity. *"One Dream,"* I say as I feel the punch-drunk embrace of gravipause as it pulls me in, pushes me away all at the same time. And I want to get up and run and keep running, but I just can't. I want to sleep, but for some reason, I can't do that either.

An unannounced rain begins to fall and Jimmie sprints for his garage, a half-painted sheep tucked under one arm, freshly coated Jesus held out like an offering. But the rain comes on and comes on strong. Balthazar and Melchior bleeding color in the drive-way, a plastic camel, all silent witnesses, as Jimmie cradles the Virgin Mary in his arms, ferries her across the wet grass to the carport where I know he will keep her, safe and dry, until the storm passes. And I feel for the first time in so many years—since I was a child, in fact—

feel as if I would cry. But I do not. No. I just lie there in my hammock, while shepherds and wise men stare blankly as I reach for words that elude me just now. Words not bound by the gravity of this moment. Words to help me put some sense to all this.

9.

Still Life With Car Seat in the Rain. 64 Nash Rambler. Metallic blue. On the corner of Bergen and heading out. He takes a drag from his cigarette, glances in the rear view mirror at the car seat lying on its side. The car seat that once kept his youngest son safe on short trips to the park or to the A & P or to the Sacred Heart where he would drop his wife off—head directly to that barstool that had become somewhat of a prosthesis—one that raised him, provided balance. And there in the dim light of Dan Ferry's Saloon he would join in the chorus of whiskey baritones, voices that were more sand then demolition, would commiserate with his fellows—other men whose calloused hands were wrapped around short glasses of beer, whose wives were now sequestered away at the Sacred Heart, bowing kerchiefed heads, whispering solemn novenas. But it was a car seat that preyed on him now—its pastel pinks and blues and dancing balloon clowns contesting the decision he had already made. He— The lover. The brawler. The father of two, soon three. The errant husband who was now stepping out of his life with the same simple effort that one usually reserves for slipping out of an old sneaker.

He takes another drag as rain makes a brief stand against the rhythmic onslaught of the wipers. The Rambler coasts to a stop. He looks around, and is grateful that Lincoln Park is empty now. No drunks on benches. Cops on the beat. Kids on the make. No mothers wiping ice cream besmirched cheeks with spit wet napkins. Just an empty park to bear witness. 7:03 in the a.m.

A matter of seconds is all it takes for him to liberate that car seat from the back of his 64, place it on a park bench solo, the soft warp of wood and chipped green paint a sad contrast to the innocent pinks and blues. A car seat in the rain, alone on a park bench, left now to fend for itself against a future that is, not unlike the sky that envelopes all Jersey City, gray and indifferent.

Coda

Music For A Sunday Morning

I remember the first time she said it. In the front seat of my Dhiatsu (*Deathtrap*) coupe, en route to the beach at Kada. She reached over with slender fingers, virtuoso fingers, and touched my knee. "Aishiteru wa," is what she said. And then she turned her face away. I remember how I felt at that very moment—my life until then a clenched fist, hard, inviolable now slowly opening to the soft music of her voice. "Aishiteru wa," is what she said. And for the first time in my life I *heard* the music—felt it.

That night we made love in my apartment, the lurid light of the Pachinko parlor across the highway blinking a steady rhythm against my bedroom wall, a subtle counter line to our own rhythm. July 6, 1992. Osaka. "Aishiteru wa," is what she said and she said it again in the morning as we lay naked and vulnerable, her head on my chest, "Aishiteru wa," and when she spoke her words pressed gently to my ears like sun against rice paper—music for a Sunday morning.

But that was eleven years ago.

Now when she speaks her words are double agents, furtive, menacing, they creep up behind me and expose me for the man I really am. The man who has perfected his own brand of subterfuge. The man who refuses as a matter of principle or primal memory to put the toilet seat down. The man who forgets her birthday but remembers to the minute when pitchers and catchers report for spring training. The man who leaves his shoes on, laughs at his own jokes, eats his rice with a spoon. The man she married eleven years ago. When she speaks now I hear the shrill discord of every wife from Jersey to Osaka. These days. When she speaks, my ears—the soft weathered wood of a railroad tie—her words like rusty spikes and tongue an ambivalent pink hammer that drives them in. These days. When she speaks I hear the sound of somebody beating Yoko Ono's cat with a large stick!!!

SUNDAY MORNING and not too long ago:

SHE SAYS: "Brian, why you gonna wear this jeans everyday? Why you doesn't put on the *clozes* which I buy for you?"

I HEAR: "O Husband. My Husband. O Girthsome one. Patron saint of pork and beans. He who has forsaken the treadmill, left it to languish in the darkest corner of our basement. He who has taken to the sofa like a pig takes to grunting. He of the baggy sweatshirt and bloated face. He whose waistline corresponds to his age and keeps on expanding. O Husband. My Husband.

I must confess that watching you dress is such great sport—the sweat down your neck, your arms trembling as you suffer to button your Levi's. O Husband. My Husband. You are truly the first Irish

American Sumo."

AND MY RESPONSE: "Honey, are we out of Taylor Ham?"

SUNDAY MORNING and not too long ago:

SHE SAYS: "Brian, when you gonna cut the grass? This house looks very embarrassing..."

I HEAR: "O Husband. My Husband. You lazy lout. You who cultivate lethargy as if it were a rare and exotic flower. And while we're on that subject, it's getting as though I need a pith helmet and Zulu guide just to navigate the perilous, verdant expanse that has become our front yard. There are dandelions the size of small trees out there and I swear when I took the trash out last night I heard something roar. O Husband. My Husband. The neighbors are getting restless. They are circulating a petition. They're calling the Board of Health. They're threatening to drop napalm, my husband. Have you no shame? I am tired of living on safari."

AND MY RESPONSE: "Honey, I think the mower is out of gas."

SUNDAY MORNING and not too long ago:

SHE SAYS: "Brian, you're not going to drink another beer, are you?"

I HEAR: "O Husband. My Husband. I realize now that because of your ancestry and genetic predisposition you harbor an insatiable appetite for that which comes in the squat brown bottles. Fruit of the hinterland. When you dream do you dream of hops and barley swaying beneath a steady sun? Bottles of Budweiser dancing to the chorus of 99 bottles of beer on the wall 99 bottles of beer if one of them bottles should happen to fall... O Husband. My Husband. I knew when I met you that you had a penchant for things frothy and golden, but I never believed in my young heart that it would come to this. My husband a full on, to the curb, Ted Kennedy, stumblebum drunk. Like father like son, I guess. O Husband. My Husband. We have so many bridges yet to cross. But I refuse to let you drag me under, my husband. I shall NOT be Kopeckne'ed!"

AND MY RESPONSE: "Honey, where in the hell is the remote control?"

SUNDAY just last week:

We decide to take a drive to the beach. Top down 70 Buick LeSabre convertible. A gentle breeze pushes dark hair from her eyes as we pull away from the house. A 30-year mortgage we share. Another bridge to cross. And she smiles at the sudden calm and at the grass that stretches its green fingers up concealing the basement windows. Quiet now but for the low ebb hum of the engine and the wind that envelops us. A welcome quiet as we head toward the Garden State Parkway. She drapes a hand across her midriff. "Aishiteru wa," she says. And when she speaks I hear the sound of water over smooth stones. Music for a Sunday morning. And I find myself reaching back, trying desperately to pull something into that front seat with us, something to remind us. Remind me. Mornings spent drinking tea in her father's garden. Her head on my chest after making love. The beach at Kada. And quiet. A quiet without edges.

Eclipse

A frequent event in space; an eclipse occurs when one planetary mass moves into the shadow of another. There are several types of eclipses in our solar system, most notably solar and lunar. A lunar eclipse occurs when the moon passes through the Earth's shadow, a solar eclipse when the moon passes between the sun and the Earth in syzygy (alignment of three or more bodies in the same gravitational strata).

She moves in apogee across the hardwood floor. Her belly beginning to show now— a crescent moon veiled in soft flannel nightshirt. And pauses before the chiffonier to glance in the mirror. I sit up in bed across from her. She turns toward me but says nothing. We are in perfect alignment. But that is misleading. Three bodies sharing the same small universe, three bodies in perfect syzygy. Father. Mother. Unborn child. Bound by gravity or some other invisible, immutable force that keeps us. And we stay, if only for a moment. The bedroom is cold, as she moves slowly past the mirror, toward the lamp, leaving each of us in shadow.

"What will we do?" she says.

"Don't know," I say, "what *will* we do?"

10.

Vitalis. My father wore Vitalis. And sometimes to extremes. And left moist shadows on pillow cases everywhere (the Rorschach of Vitalis), and spat on subway platforms directly below the sign that read:

NO SPITTING
$100 FINE
NYPD

He was a complicated man. My father. And could fall asleep in any number of interesting positions. Once, as a child, I asked him, "Where do you go when you die?"

"Secaucus," he answered without opening his eyes.

So this chapter is dedicated to Vitalis. The hair it claimed sovereignty over, oily crown and indelible imprint that it left behind.

(My father also owned a stainless steel comb that he would wield on Sundays before mass or at the outset of family gatherings. On the morning he left, he left that comb behind. Also, put an unopened bottle of 4 Roses in the refrigerator. Don't ask me to explain this. I guess it's just one of those things, ya know?)

Launch

Idling at the light in my 70 Buick LeSabre. Ragtop down. A Stinger F1M-surface to air missile strapped across my back. McDonald's Happy Meal between my legs. It's June 8, 2004, and Venus is in transit. Vagrant beauty mark across the yellow face of the sun. Another eclipse.

And they say that this is a rare celestial spectacle. That the last time this phenomenon was visible to the naked eye was 1822. And I know that Venus is the Roman goddess of love and beauty and fertility and spring. And I know that right now my wife is probably selecting curtains for the nursery or is being recruited by a stop-at-nothing, stiff-nippled operative from the Le Leche League.

But I'm stuck in traffic, radio off as I try to feel the rhythm of my own life, while Venus makes her move. And I'd like to report that my wife's last sonogram went well (it did) and that this pregnancy has brought us much closer together, and that our unborn child—who, by the way, is a boy—will somehow save us. But I can't. I just don't know. The only thing that I *can* be sure of right now is that I am stuck. Thinking of staying. Or leaving. My wife and unborn son. Allison. And my father, wondering what *he* was thinking that morning, all those years ago. And it occurs to me that I am probably the only person in this whole wide galaxy who, at this very moment, has Venus fixed in his crosshairs as she makes a move on an unsuspecting sun. Venus. The goddess of love. A myth, I am told. I am taking aim. I'm getting ready to launch.

Acknowledgements

I am forever grateful to the following people for their encouragement and patience over the years and for picking up my tab when I truly had nothing left.

My mother, Margaret *Maggie Jigs* Bradford, wife Sadako, and daughter Erin—you save my life. Day in. Day out. Nan, Pop, and Uncle Warren. My brother Terry who once said I was the smartest guy in the room (I believe we were standing in a phone booth at the time), and the Bradfords of Denman Place. Paul "Hop" Hopkins, dice devotee, dreamer, fellow pilgrim on this journey. My family on the other side, Okada Kiyomi, Mutsoyoshi, and Mayuko. Willie. Christian "Doc" Tatu, no one I'd rather be marooned with in the wee smalls—stoop at Mother's, Naw'lins. Friends and colleagues: Karen Hillyer, Kerry Frabizio, Rose Lynch, Dennis and Kim, Cinders, Jaci and 107—the good angels. Nut, Jerry Ingram, Ol' Man Phil, Terry O, Drewskie, and Tim *Bollocks* Round—the not so good angels. My mentors at CU and FDU especially you, Ellen Akins, your guidance has made all the difference. Thank you Jaded Ibis Press and Debra Di Blasi for your courage and vision and willingness to take risks. And Cheryl Heinlen—we never had a chance to get that one last drink at the Parrot—I miss you, old friend, and think of those days often.

Special thanks to BJ Ward—Scourge of the Gulf Stream. Scoundrel. Equal parts Cuban leaf, single malt scotch and Bobby Kennedy. Back is got. Wagon fixed. Buddy Boy, you continue to amaze and inspire!

About the Author

A recipient of the Henfield Transatlantic Review Award for Fiction, **Brian Bradford** has published work in numerous small press publications including: *New Blood* and *Black Ice* (FC2). He holds an MFA in Creative Writing from Fairleigh Dickinson University. and teaches at Warren County Community College, where he is a full professor and co-director of the Creative Writing Program. When not teaching or writing, you will find him in his laboratory working diligently to create environmentally friendly foot deodorants for our astronauts and Olympic Athletes. He currently resides in New Jersey with his wife Sadako, daughter Erin, two Cavapoo, and an empty birdcage.

www.ingramcontent.com/pod-product-compliance
Lightning Source LLC
Chambersburg PA
CBHW020704260626
47157CB00008B/3137